Maid for the Doms

S L Davies

Published by S L Davies, 2022.

MAID FOR THE DOMS

First edition. December 5, 2022.

Copyright © 2022 S L Davies.

ISBN: 979-8215773284

Written by S L Davies.

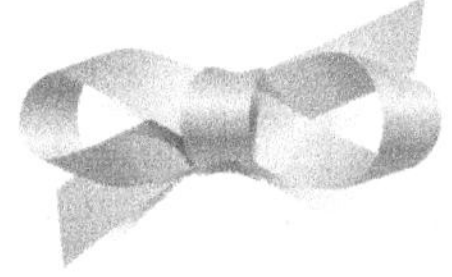

Chapter One

Alaina stood in front of the huge wrought iron gates that led to the imposing white stone mansion. She chewed on her bottom lip wondering whether she really needed a job that badly. Maybe she could go back to the club, maybe she could beg Frankie for her old job back, she could even promise that she wouldn't punch another customer who grabbed her ass. Shaking her head, Alaina reached out with a trembling finger and pressed the buzzer beside the gate and waited.

Her heart was beating out of her chest, the longer she stood there the more she wanted to flee. Looking around, Alaina knew it would be a long walk back into town. Her uber driver had continued to check with her that this is where she wanted to go. Now she wished she had told him to take her back. Alaina wished she had told him that she had the wrong address.

"Yes?" a deep voice barked through the crackling speaker, causing Alaina to startle.

"Um, hi, my name is Alaina, I'm the new housekeeper?" she said kicking herself for the way her voice trembled with nerves.

Alaina's best friend Kelsey told her she was crazy to take the job without meeting her bosses. However, the agency that she had, had the interview with, assured her that the pay would be good and the fact that she was going to be able to live in the home was a bonus. She couldn't continue to sleep on Kelsey's couch and there was no way that she was going to go back to her parent's house. That would feel too much like failure.

The gate groaned as it started to swing open. She took a deep breath and started up the long-paved driveway towards the house. The gardens

1

were perfectly manicured. All Alaina knew about her new bosses was that they were twin recluses and were very particular about how their home was to be run. When she tried googling their names, the most she could find was that Cash and Morrisey Caldwell were the owners of one of the biggest tech companies in the world. There were no photos of them, and from all reports that she read they had never been seen in public.

That should have been enough to turn Alaina away, but after being fired from her job at the club, because she punched one of the locals in the cock, after he grabbed her ass one too many times, and then being kicked out of her house because she couldn't afford the rent, she was desperate. When the agency told her that this job would pay her more money than she could even envision and she would have the opportunity to live in a mansion, she jumped in with both feet.

Now she was walking to the front door of the mansion to meet her future bosses that she knew nothing about. Nerves swirled around her stomach when she finally reached the large marble porch and went to the front door that stood open. Alaina bit her lip questioning whether she should just walk in or wait to be greeted.

"Are you coming in or not? I've got things to do today," a gruff voice growled at her from just beyond the door where the shadows hid the man's face.

"Sorry," Alaina murmured before going through the door and shutting it with a soft click behind her.

When she turned to see the man that had spoken, her breath was stolen from her lungs. He was not only the biggest man she had ever seen, but he was also one of the most handsome men. He had dark hair that was cut short on the sides but left long on top with a slight curl. His eyes were a startling green that looked up and down Alaina, taking in every inch of her. When he finally got to her face, he narrowed his eyes and frowned slightly. He couldn't have been more than thirty years old. She had assumed that the twins were elderly men. Shaking her head, she came to the quick conclusion that the man before her, wasn't either Cash or Morrisey.

"You are younger than I was expecting," he huffed.

Alaina raised her brow and put her hands on her hips, "sorry to disappoint, I am who the agency felt was the best for the job," she replied sharply.

The man folded his arms across his expansive chest, the movement bulged his biceps, he was intimidating, from the size of him to the angry glare that he bore into her. Alaina wanted to turn and run but locked her knees to prevent from moving.

"Anyway, I'm here to work for Mr.'s Caldwell, are they here?" she asked.

The man continued to glare at her, his eyes widening slightly, before the corner of his lips twitched in a small smirk. He turned on his heel and walked away, leaving Alaina standing in the grand foyer with her mouth dropped open.

"For fucks sake," she growled as she dropped her bag at her feet. Alaina wasn't looking forward to working alongside that man at all. He was an arrogant ass and she just hoped that her new bosses were better than him.

She stood at the base of the stairs looking around the foyer, going over in her mind what she should do. The room that she was in was opulence to the extreme, the floor was a highly polished marble, expensive artwork and statues were dotted through the room, and an imposing grand staircase wound its way up to a second floor. When Alaina looked up the stairs, she saw a man standing at the top looking down at her, with a curious expression. She didn't know how long he had been observing her, but seeing him standing there with a look of wry mirth on his face and his arms folded across his chest, made her wonder if he had witnessed her interaction with the man previous

Alaina's mouth dropped open, she wondered what the hell was in the water, the only two men she had seen, were gorgeous. This man was just as tall and broad as the other, but where the other had almost black hair, this man's hair was lighter, and long past his shoulders. He was too far away to see the color of his eyes, but he watched her with the same keen interest as the other man.

"Ah hello, my name is Alaina, I am meant to be starting here today as the new housekeeper. I'm wondering if you could possibly introduce me to either of the Mr.'s Caldwell's?" she asked, after staring in lust for longer than what would have been polite.

The man at the top of the stairs cocked his head to the side before moving towards her, with a grace that made him appear to float rather than walk. "My brother didn't take you to your room. Or show you what we expect of you?" he asked with a frown.

When he reached the bottom step and walked closer to her, it was then that she noticed the same startling green eyes of the man that she had first met, "you are Mr. Caldwell?" she asked.

The man smirked slightly before nodding his head briefly. Alaina kicked herself silently, not five minutes in the door and she had made a complete fool of herself, no wonder the other man, whichever Caldwell brother he was, looked at her like she was ridiculous. In her defense, she had tried to see what they looked like and couldn't find a single picture online. She didn't even know their ages, nothing. So, it wasn't completely unreasonable for her to assume that the brothers were crazy old billionaires.

"I am Cash, and you I assume, have already met my brother Morrisey, if you follow me, I'll take you to your room and then give you a rundown of what we expect from you here," he said before he turned and walked down the same hallway that Morrisey had gone.

Cash led Alaina to a large bedroom on the ground floor. The room had a huge window that looked out towards the back of the property that was surrounded by woods. In the center of the room was the biggest bed she had ever seen, with luxurious quilts and pillows. The whole room continued that opulent feel of the house.

"This is your bedroom, through there," Cash said pointing towards a door, "is a wardrobe and your ensuite."

Alaina looked around the room in shock, she couldn't believe what she was seeing. It was the fanciest home she had ever lived, even as a child she never experienced anything like this. Her parents weren't wealthy, just simple working class. Never in her wildest dreams would she have envisioned living in such a lap of luxury. When she looked back at Cash, she noticed him watching her with bemusement.

"You can leave your belongings here for the moment and we will go over what is expected of you," he said, before he turned and walked from the room.

Alaina left her bags beside the bed and followed to where Cash was waiting . As he led her through the house he continued to point out various rooms, such as the laundry and the guest rooms, which he said weren't used on a regular basis, however, she was expected to keep them cleaned and prepare them when they did host.

Once they reached the second floor of the grand house, Cash pointed out his bedroom, followed by Morrisey's. "We will leave our laundry in the baskets for you to do each day, our bathrooms are to be cleaned every day as are our bedrooms, we expect fresh linen on the beds," Cash explained.

Alaina nodded her head, taking note of everything he was directing her to do, hoping that she could remember everything. She wished that she had brought a note pad to write down Cash's instructions. He continued to lead her throughout the home, pointing out other guest rooms, before they got to the office spaces.

Alaina's eyes widened as she looked around the room at the various computer screens that dotted the wall. Some played news programs on silent, and others had the stock exchange constantly running. Morrisey was sitting behind a huge mahogany desk typing away. When they entered the room, he leaned back in his chair and put his hands behind his head, smirking at Alaina.

She narrowed her eyes at him, wanting to give him a piece of her mind for not simply telling her who he was. Morrisey raised an eyebrow in challenge and Alaina bit down any scolding words that were forming. Morrisey smirked again, wearing a look of victory while Cash continued with instructions, oblivious to Alaina and his brother's silent exchange.

"This is where we do our work from and where we spend most of our time. We don't expect you to clean in here. However, in here contains very sensitive information. You may see things that our competition desperately wants to get their hands on," Cash said looking at her with narrowed eyes, "and believe me if they get their hands on our work, we will know that it comes from you, and if that happens, we will ruin you."

Alaina nodded her head emphatically letting him know that they could trust her. There was a chance that she didn't understand anything that was contained in the room however, she also understood the importance of trust. She wanted this job, she was relying on this job, without it she would be homeless. She needed the brothers to be able to trust her. Alaina wouldn't sell them out to anyone.

"Good, so every day at twelve we expect lunch to be brought to us here, we eat dinner at six and breakfast at eight in the morning. You will oversee the preparation of all meals," Cash continued.

Alaina was starting to feel overwhelmed. She knew that she was a decent cook, but these brothers were so wealthy, what if they were used to five-star quality meals? What if she couldn't do all that was expected of her.

"You are overwhelming her," Morrisey said from behind his desk, seeming to easily pick up on Alaina's struggles.

Cash looked over his shoulder at his brother before turning his attention towards Alaina again with a frown, "are you going to be able to do this job? Because if you can't, you need to tell me now," he said.

Alaina shook her head, "no, I'm sorry, I can do the job, I'm trying to remember everything, if I could just write it down, I feel that would help."

"Of course," Cash said, turning to his desk and rummaging around the various papers that were strewn across it before holding a pen and paper out to her, "here you go, do you need me to go over everything again?"

Alaina shook her head, and quickly jotted down everything that she was told, noting the mealtimes and what was expected of her regarding cleaning. When she had everything written down, she looked back up at the brothers and gave them a smile.

"Okay, that's everything," she said.

Cash gave her a single nod of his head, before he waved his hand for her to follow as he left the room and continued to lead her throughout the house. Alaina followed Cash along the second floor until they got to a room that had a door that was shut. Cash stopped in front of the door and crossed his arms across his chest.

"This room, you are not to enter, this is our private room, so you under no circumstances are allowed in there, do you understand me?" he asked.

Alaina's curiosity was peaked, she couldn't be told not to go somewhere and not wonder what the secret was, but she nodded in agreement that she wouldn't enter the room. Her mind was wracked with ideas of what could be behind the door, from a dungeon to a safe where they kept their riches.

When Cash seemed satisfied that she understood everything and had written down what was expected of her, he dismissed her for the rest of the day, until she had to prepare their meals. Alaina went back to her room so that she could unpack her belongings. When she entered the bathroom, she looked longingly at the bath and wondered if she had time to take a long soak before she had to make the brothers dinner.

Alaina couldn't remember how long it had been since she had soaked in a bath, never since she left her parents home at eighteen.

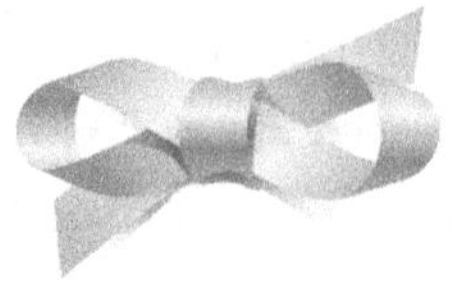

Chapter Two

Alaina was searching through the fridge for the ingredients to prepare the men their meal. They had food that Alaina didn't even have the tiniest bit of knowledge about. She wasn't a bad cook, it's just that she hadn't ever had the money or experience in cooking with caviar or whatever kind of fish john dory was. She felt like she was somewhat out of her depth.

One of the first things she thought she would have to do was to start buying some cookbooks so that she could prepare better meals for the brothers. She didn't know who had been doing their meal prep before she came along, but she wanted to make sure that she prepared things that weren't just edible but delicious. However, for now they were going to have to put up with simple dishes.

Alaina pulled out the ingredients for spaghetti bolognaise with meatballs. She hoped that they liked Italian food. It was one of the few things that she was good at cooking. Looking at the clock on the wall she wondered if she would have enough time to make the pasta from scratch, or whether they would even notice the difference.

The smell of the bolognaise sauce was making her mouth water. Cash hadn't discussed with her what the rules were around her eating. She assumed that she would be allowed to eat meals, but as to whether that was to happen with the brothers or not, she wasn't sure. She decided that she would make a plate up for herself and eat in the kitchen, if they requested her to eat with them, then she would join them.

"That smells divine," Cash said from behind her. Alaina turned and gave him a bright smile.

"Thank you, I wasn't sure if you would like Italian food or not, without cookbooks, I'm afraid I'm limited on what recipes I remember," she explained.

"Of course, come with me," Cash said, as he led her from the kitchen into a small alcove, that almost looked like a walk-in pantry. He pushed open the cupboard door and stacked inside was a mountain load of cookbooks.

Alaina's eyes widened as she took in the stacks of books, from celebrity chefs, to local restaurant chefs, there was books there for every cuisine and every event. She was practically salivating with the thought of the various meals she could conjure up.

"Oh wow, this is amazing," she exclaimed, "I can't wait to prep up a meal plan and then start cooking."

"I look forward to eating what you create," Cash said with a chuckle before he turned and left the room, leaving Alaina to continue staring over the various books.

By the time she came back to the kitchen, the water had just started boiling for the pasta and she saw that she had fifteen minutes before the brother's would be ready for their meals. Alaina busied herself finishing off the pasta and serving it up with a side of garlic bread and a garden salad. When she brought the meal to the table, Cash and Morrisey were sitting waiting. They were both dressed in jeans and a fresh t-shirt, they both looked like they had showered. Alaina couldn't believe how beautiful both men were. She shook herself as she continued to bring the brother's meals to the table, checking herself so as not to be caught drooling over her bosses.

When Alaina sat the dish in front of Cash he bent forward and sniffed at his plate, "this smells beautiful, I'm looking forward to digging in," he said with a bright smile.

Alaina set the dish in front of Morrisey, before placing the salad in the center of the table. "I hope you enjoy," she said with a bright smile, before turning to leave the room. She planned to plate herself a dish and eat it in the kitchen.

"Alaina, why don't you bring a plate of food for yourself and sit with us, we would like to chat with you and get to know you better," Cash said.

Alaina looked between the two, she bit her lip, unsure what the right move was. She didn't know if this was a test and she should politely decline the offer, however, if Cash truly wanted to get to know her, it would be rude if she did decline the offer.

"I promise we won't bite, well not unless you ask us to," Cash said with a small chuckle.

Alaina smiled before nodding her head, she left the dining room and gathered her plate of spaghetti bolognaise and some cutlery and going back to sit down at the table. The brother's watched her as she sat opposite Morrisey, with Cash at the head of the table. Once she was seated, Cash and Morrisey picked up their cutlery and began to eat. Alaina followed suit and started in on her meal. It was her best one yet, she figured it helped having the finest of ingredients to work with, rather than whatever was on sale.

"Alaina, tell us about yourself?" Morrisey said as he dabbed his mouth with a napkin.

Alaina finished the mouthful of food that she had before answering, "I'm not sure what I can tell you, I'm twenty-five years old, I grew up with my parents. My dad worked in the glass factory and my mum was a commercial cleaner. I have two older brothers; one is in the military and the other is a chef."

"Why didn't you go to college?" Morrisey asked.

Alaina dropped her head; she was ashamed that she never had the chance to go to college. She had applied for every scholarship that had become available, but her grades just weren't good enough. She had been diagnosed with dyslexia when she was twelve years old. She had always struggled with school, getting good grades didn't come easily like it did for her brother Trenton. He just seemed to sail through school, but for

Alaina it was something she struggled with. The words would jump all over the page and numbers appeared backwards. Her parents tried to help as much as they could, but money was limited, her parents worked hard to keep a roof over their heads and food on the table, there wasn't a lot of spare money for therapists and specialized tutors. So, Alaina had to simply muddle through.

"There wasn't enough money to pay for college," she said quietly.

"Did your brother's go to college?" Cash asked.

Alaina shook her head, "Trenton, who is the chef, he went to culinary school after working for a year in a restaurant and being sponsored by his boss. My older brother Zeb joined the military when he was eighteen and had just graduated high school. I tried to get scholarships, but because of my dyslexia I couldn't get an academic scholarship and I didn't play sport," she said with a shrug of her shoulder.

"What would you have done if you had got a scholarship?" Morrisey asked.

Alaina sat back and thought about the question, "I think I would have done something creative, I love to draw and paint, so I would have possibly done something in the arts."

"I would love to see some of your drawings some time," Cash said to her.

Alaina smiled. "I would be honored to show you. I imagine I'm not as good as others, but it is something I have loved to do for years."

"Don't do that," Morrisey said with a stern look. Alaina was confused what he meant, did he mean for her not to show Cash her artwork? "Don't compare yourself to others. Art is subjective. Just because I love a piece of art and it makes me feel a certain way, doesn't mean that Cash doesn't hate it. So, don't compare yourself to other artists."

Alaina nodded, "I will try not to, sir," she promised, ducking her head as he chastised her.

She heard Morrisey's chair push out from the table. Alaina continued to look down at her plate, her face blushed with embarrassment after being told off for comparing herself to other's. She never felt she was smart enough, pretty enough or good enough as others. Her self-esteem had hit an all-time low when she was seventeen and her mother had caught Alaina cutting into her thigh with an old rusty razor blade. Her mother never screamed or yelled, even though Alaina was sure she wanted to. Instead she had cleaned Alaina's thigh up, and calmly took her into the kitchen where she put the kettle on and made them both a cup of tea. Her mother then proceeded to ask Alaina to tell her everything that led up to the point, where she felt she had to cut herself.

There was so many tears and snot flowing through the conversation as Alaina filled her mum in on the bullying that she was facing from kids at school. The boy who had asked her out only to follow it up with laughter and humiliation when she said yes. The bullying could only happen so many times before she couldn't take it anymore. When Trenton found out about the boy, who had been the catalyst for her wanting to self-harm, he left the house in a hurry, his eyes angry and jaw clenched. When he got home that night, he had grazed knuckles and a black eye. That was nothing in comparison to what the three boys that had humiliated Alaina at school the previous day looked like. Their eyes were all swollen shut and they had split lips. The boy who had instigated her humiliation had a broken nose and a cut on his eyebrow that was stitched.

The boys although they never apologized to her, they never bothered her again after that. Alaina flinched when she felt Morrisey's fingers cup her chin and slowly lift her face to him. "Alaina, you are perfect the way you are. It doesn't matter that you have dyslexia, it doesn't change the beauty that you are. I don't want you to compare yourself to others because all that does is bring you down. Remember everyone has faults. Look at any celebrity, they are beautiful on the outside, but how many of them are drug addicts, how many of them are desperately lonely or are raging alcoholics? Everyone has faults Alaina. But sometimes what we view as faults, are attributes to what makes us the perfect people we are. Do you understand?" he asked.

Alaina nodded her head. She did understand. She had been told for years by her family that she wasn't stupid. Having dyslexia didn't make her a fool, or an idiot. She wasn't dumb. Sure, she had trouble reading because of the way that the letters and numbers would jump over the page, but that didn't mean she was stupid either.

"Thank you," she said quietly, lowering her eyes back to her plate.

When she looked up again Morrisey and Cash were watching her with a fire in their eyes, that she couldn't understand. The only time men had looked at her like that, meant they wanted her body. She hadn't given that piece of herself over to anyone. She wasn't holding onto it for a reason, she just hadn't found the man that she wanted enough to get naked with. However, sitting at the table with the Caldwell brothers' eyes on her she struggled to sit still. A fire was being lit between her legs and it was a fire that maybe only they could quench.

Morrisey cleared his throat and nodded. "Right, well I've got a bit of work left to do. So, I'll leave you to it. Thank you for dinner Alaina, it was delicious, I look forward to eating more of your food," he said with a smile, that didn't show any of the mistrust and what seemed like dislike that had covered his face when they had first met.

Alaina smiled back at him and stood, watching both he and Cash leave the table. She started to collect up the dirty dishes to take to the kitchen as she pondered what it was that had just transpired between the three of them. She knew that she shouldn't even be thinking the way she was, these men were her bosses. If anything happened between them, it would be highly inappropriate. However, she couldn't seem to convince her brain or her vagina of that. At that moment her brain was still relishing over Morrisey's soft touch on her jaw and her vagina was dripping with fantasies of what else those fingers could do.

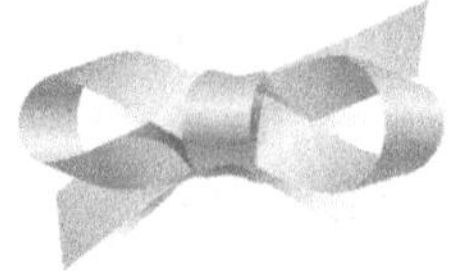

Chapter Three

After Alaina had finished cleaning the dinner dishes and the kitchen, she spent the rest of her night tucked up in bed, pouring over recipes that she could cook for the Caldwell brother's. There were so many dishes she wanted to try and now that she had access to the ingredients it gave her the opportunity to branch out beyond basic meals.

When Alaina's alarm had gone off at seven, she was awake with a new sense of excitement for what her day would bring. The first being another meal. This time breakfast. She decided to go with the traditional, English breakfast, until she got an understanding of what the brothers liked to eat, she didn't want to get too creative with their meals.

Alaina had set up the table as she did for dinner the previous night and waited for the brothers to arrive at eight o'clock before setting their breakfast in front of them. This time she wasn't asked to join, so Alaina ate quietly in the kitchen. When she finished, she went back into the dining room and noticed that both the brothers had left the table, plates cleaned of food and empty.

Disappointment flooded Alaina; she had hoped to have the opportunity to be able to get to know the brothers more. She thought maybe the spark of interest they showed her last night meant something. She couldn't help that niggling sadness that crept into her heart. Alaina shook her head and took in a deep breath.

She couldn't see them as any more than her bosses and she felt silly for allowing such an idea to even start to grow. All she could do was start her day and get on with the job that they were paying her to do. Alaina wondered if the night before had been a test. All she could hope for is that she had passed.

Morrisey

God damn that woman was beautiful. Her long dark hair that she had pinned up in a ballerina bun on top of her head, her long legs and that gorgeous body that she hid under baggy clothes. He couldn't believe that Alaina saw herself as anything but the desirable woman she was. It had broken his heart last night when she told them about her having dyslexia and therefore not feeling like she was as good as others.

He wanted to burn the world down, just to show her that she was perfect. It took everything in him, not to take her over his knee and spank her bottom red, until she realized how gorgeous she was. And then she went and called him sir. His cock had hardened immediately. He wanted her desperately but had to show some control. Morrisey's jaw had been aching as he walked away with the strength that he was clenching his teeth. The girl was here as their housekeeper, she was not their pet.

It had been so long since Cash and he had shared a girl in that capacity. Sure, they had their parties, and they had their nights of pleasure. However, it was something else to have that one woman who was willing to give herself over and become completely submissive to them both. Allowing them to take control of her entire pleasure and life. The last woman that he and Cash shared had broken Cash's heart.

It still made Morrisey curl his lip in a snarl when he thought about what that bitch had done. Cash had given her his whole heart and she had torn it from him, chewed it up and spat it back out. Cash had plans to marry her, he wanted to have children with her. Morrisey loved her too, but he was a lot more guarded with his heart than Cash was. However, Amanda had stolen everything from Cash when he caught her in bed, with another man. Apparently, she had never been faithful to the brothers. She was just in it for what she could get out of them. When she got bored, she decided it was time to move on. Instead of just telling

Cash and Morrisey that she no longer wanted them, she made sure Cash caught her with someone else.

Cash didn't eat or sleep for weeks, they made a hell of a lot of money in that time, because all Cash did was work. Eventually his heart started to heal, and his heart ache turned to anger, before it turned to mistrust of women. It was why when Morrisey had organized a new housekeeper after Lola retired, he asked for an older woman, someone motherly, and less likely to be sexually attractive and untrustworthy. Instead the agency sent Alaina. Beauty personified.

When they went to their office after breakfast, Cash looked uncomfortable and somewhat more stressed than normal. He tended to always be tightly strung, but this was something new. Morrisey knew the cause, he was just waiting to see what Cash would say.

"She can't work here," Cash blurted.

Morrisey sighed and reached out giving his brothers shoulder a squeeze. "The agency sent her because they felt she could do the job. Do you believe she can't do the job?"

"No, that's not it," Cash sighed with a shake of his head, "I think she can do the job, but my god, you saw how naturally submissive she is. You can see with your own two eyes how fucking gorgeous she is. My cock has been hard since the minute I saw her standing in the foyer."

Morrisey chuckled, he understood Cash's problem, his cock had instantly hardened the minute he had seen her. "So, what do you propose we do? Fire her? For what reason? You know the agency isn't going to send someone else, just because we fired Alaina on the grounds that she made our dicks hard."

"I know, I know," Cash said as he ran his hands up over his face, "I just don't want to go back there Morrisey, I don't want to revisit that time."

Morrisey leaned forward so that he was looking into Cash's eyes, "Alaina isn't Amanda. She is just our employee. Amanda started as our girlfriend; she didn't work for us. So, we treat Alaina as an employee only. When was the last time you got laid?"

Cash looked at Morrisey sheepishly and shrugged his shoulder, "I don't know, the last party we had I think, and even then Autumn had her damned claws in my arm the whole fucking night, that it was just a quick fuck with that blonde Amazonian woman, what was her name?"

"Jesus, Cash," Morrisey barked out a laugh, "you can't call her an Amazonian woman, her name is Breanna, she's a model for crying out loud."

Cash shrugged his shoulder, "she's huge, not my type."

"Why did you go there then?" Morrisey asked raising an eyebrow and shaking his head.

"She was the one closest and easiest to sneak out with, without Autumn noticing. Fuck that woman annoys the hell out of me. Why she can't go and find any other man in the damned room, why always me?"

"She has always had a thing for you Cash. What if we organize another party, just a small affair, without Autumn?" Morrisey suggested.

"Do you think Alaina would be up to organizing one of our parties?" Cash asked raising an eyebrow at his brother.

"Only one way to find out," Morrisey said as he picked his phone out of his pocket and rang down to Alaina's number.

"Hello?" she answered on the second ring.

"Alaina, could you come up to the office please?" Morrisey asked.

"Sure thing, I'll be right up," she said sounding a little nervous and unsure. Her tone made Morrisey smile. Hanging up the phone he sat down at his desk and waited.

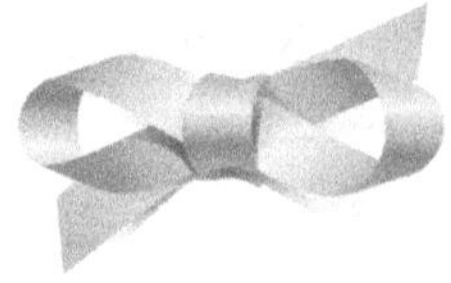

Chapter Four

Alaina could feel her nervousness rising as she went up the stairs to the office space. She had just finished putting on the laundry and was about to put new sheets on the brother's beds, when Morrisey's phone call came in. Alaina worried that they were about to fire her. She questioned everything she had said to them, had she done something wrong? Chewing on her lip, she knocked on the door of the office and waited for Cash or Morrisey to call out to her to enter.

"Come in," a deep voice who Alaina believed belonged to Morrisey called out.

Alaina opened the door and entered the cluttered office. Cash was sitting at his desk typing at his computer, while Morrisey was lounged out on a couch that sat against a window.

"You needed to speak to me?" Alaina said with a trembling voice. She felt ridiculous, she was strong enough to punch a patron at her last job in the dick for grabbing her ass, yet something about the Caldwell brothers intimidated her so much that she became a meek mouse around them. Tears prickled at her eyes and she blinked rapidly to prevent herself from crying.

Alaina bit her lip and frowned, as she silently cursed herself out for being so weak in front of these men. They were no different to Frankie, her last boss, or her brothers who she could speak her mind in front of without a problem. She needed to get her shit together and be strong.

"Yes, we are planning to have a party and we are wondering if you would be able to organize it for us. We will take care of the invitations, but we will need finger foods that will be served throughout the night," Morrisey said.

Alaina bit her bottom lip and sighed with relief. She wasn't going to lose her job, but this was a big test for her. She knew that she could prepare a party, that wasn't the hard part. The part that had her nervous was the fact that these men didn't just have parties like her family. They didn't just fire up a grill and start barbecuing meat and serve beer. This party would be high class and Alaina worried that she wouldn't be able to stack up to their needs. She feared she would look stupid. Alaina couldn't take the humiliation that might come with messing this up.

"There is something you need to be aware of for our parties," Cash said turning from the computer to look at Alaina, "they aren't the normal parties that people have. At these parties, you will see people who have a high standing in society, there will be judges, politicians and sports people here. These people come to our parties, to partake in something specific that we offer."

Alaina frowned as her mind went through all the things that Cash could be talking about, was there going to be drugs or illegal dealings. Alaina wouldn't be able to stay if that was the case. It was one thing having a party with a difference, but if the brothers expected her to start doing illegal shit, then she was out.

"We live somewhat of an alternative lifestyle Alaina," Morrisey said as he leaned forward in his chair, before quickly standing up, "in fact instead of just telling you what we do, come with me and I'll show you."

Alaina shook her head, she didn't want to follow Morrisey, suddenly fear spread through her, and she found herself rooted to the spot. "You are safe, little finch, I won't do anything to hurt you," Morrisey said into her ear causing goose pimples to break out over her skin. Alaina bit her tongue to prevent the groan that wanted to escape, just from the sound of his voice.

She squeezed her thighs together; these men were going to be the death of her. She never thought she had much of a sex drive, she didn't have a need to masturbate like others. When Kelsey and her other friends talked about mind blowing orgasms, Alaina couldn't participate. She had never had one. She tried, Kelsey encouraged her to buy a vibrator, but Alaina just found it more irritating rather than causing some great orgasm, so she gave up and didn't bother using it. Alaina finally threw it out when she left her apartment to move into the Caldwell mansion.

"Come, follow me," Morrisey said quietly.

Alaina nodded and although fear was flowing through her blood, her feet had other ideas, and followed him obediently. Morrisey led her down the hallway until they were out the front of the door that Cash had told her not to enter. Morrisey looked over his shoulder to see that she was still behind him and gave her a small smirk, before swinging the door open and entering the room.

The room could only be described as sultry, the walls were painted a dark grey, there was mirrors on the roof, the floor was a highly polished black marble. Standing in the middle of the room was a giant wooden cross, that looked like an X. On one wall was an array of whips, hand cuffs and feather boas as well as what looked like a milking machine that you would put on a cow. Alaina's eyes widened as she took the room in. At the back of the room was black leather couches. Underneath the milking machine was what looked like a day bed or large loveseat.

"What is this?" Alaina asked, looking up at Morrisey who was watching her closely.

"This is what our lifestyle consists of," he said casting his arm around the room, "Cash and I like control, and that flows into our sexual habits."

"You like to hurt people during sex?" she asked with a frown.

Morrisey chuckled and shook his head, "not really, pain when it is delivered properly and carefully can cause pleasure. A spanking on the bottom, or having one's nipples clamped, can make the result so much bigger. Do you understand?"

"Not really no. I... I haven't had much experience so no I don't understand," she admitted.

"Ah, I see, do you mind me asking what experience you have?" Morrisey asked.

Alaina looked up at him and noticed the fire in his eyes that he had the night before. She felt a blush creep up her neck and over her cheeks. Did she really want to admit to her boss that she had only ever kissed one boy and found it so disgusting she never went back for seconds? The way that Tyler stuck his tongue down her throat in the eighth grade made her nearly vomit. She dumped him the next day and never dated again.

"I um, nothing, I have no experience at all. I've kissed one boy in the eighth grade," she said quietly.

Morrisey raised an eyebrow but continued to watch her. Alaina felt like his stare was boring into her and stripping her naked. She felt like she should be uncomfortable under the weight of his stare, but the opposite happened, she was so turned on she squeezed her thighs together. Morrisey stepped forward into her space and dipped his face close to hers.

"Do I turn you on, Alaina?" he said low, his voice was deep and husky with need.

Alaina couldn't control the moan that escaped her throat. Slowly Morrisey slid his finger up her arm to her shoulder, leaving goose bumps in its wake. God, she wanted him, but this was her boss, damn it, her boss. She couldn't lose this job. Alaina cleared her throat, closing her eyes she took a purposeful step back. The loss of Morrisey's body heat and the scent of his aftershave made her want to step back into him, but Alaina forced herself to keep a level head. She had to think about her job.

"So, this party, will be about what you do here?" she asked, forcing herself to look at her boss and bring the topic back to the one at hand.

Morrisey gave her a wry grin and nodded his head, the fire was still dancing in his eyes as he watched her struggle with her decision to focus on work.

"Yes. There will be women here, who like to play with the men that enjoy this lifestyle too. You can expect about fifteen people. We will meet in here; some use our toys and others will bring their own. Most will be partnered and willing to play. We will expect finger foods and champagne to be readily available to our guests throughout the night."

"I can make sure that your party is catered. I will start a list of everything I need to make and do. What day are you wanting the party?" she asked, gritting her teeth against the irrational jealousy that was raging through her system. She wanted to be tied up with the silk ropes that hung from the roof. She wanted to be touched like she knew the women who were coming to the Caldwell's party would be touched.

"Friday night," Morrisey said breaking through her inner thoughts.

"Very well, I can do that. Is there something that you specifically would like to be served?" she asked.

"No, whatever you make will be fine. Thank you, Alaina," Morrisey said with another smile, before turning and leaving her alone in his room of torture.

Alaina took one more look around the room before she turned and left, heading back to the bedrooms to make beds and clean bathrooms. Her mind was going to be on what she had seen, felt and heard for the rest of the day, but she had to keep in mind that she was no more than an employee to the brothers. They could have any number of women they wanted, from wealthy backgrounds, that would complement them and their lifestyles. Someone like Alaina just wasn't meant to be for a man like Morrisey or Cash.

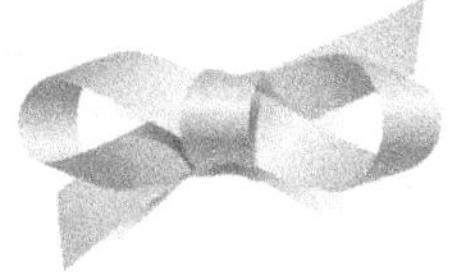

Chapter Five

Morrisey

A virgin, and not just that, one that had only kissed one guy, and that was when she was a damned teenager. Morrisey remembered his first kiss, it was fucking awful. All tongue and slobber. If he thought his dick couldn't get any harder, he was wrong. The minute that he saw the visible reaction she had to his presence, it nearly brought him to his knees. He wanted to tear her clothes from her body and pinken her ass with his hand or maybe a paddle. He knows that she would be scared, but that is what makes it more exciting.

When Morrisey went back to the office, Cash was still looking at his computer screen, pretending that Morrisey wasn't there. Finally, Cash couldn't hold back anymore and looked over at his brother. Whatever was on Morrisey's face caused Cash to snort.

"Look at you, you are so smug, what happened?" Cash asked.

Morrisey chuckled and shook his head, "she is the one, there is no if, buts or maybes about it, Cash. She is perfect. She is a virgin; she has kissed one guy in the eighth grade. That is the limit of her sexual experience, Cash."

Cash's eyes widened at the information. Morrisey knew his brother's interest would have been piqued with the knowledge that Alaina was a virgin. It was his fetish. He loved virgins. Cash loved to break them in. Whereas Morrisey liked to push them and teach them how far they could go and still find pleasure. He liked playing with wax, whips and electrodes. Cash was gentler. Together they seemed to make the perfect pair, they evened each other out. Morrisey knew that together they could teach Alaina the pleasure of their world and she would be ruined for any other man.

The only problem was that Cash would need to learn to trust her. There was also the little matter of the fact that Alaina was their employee. That made things slightly more difficult, but it was nothing they couldn't work around. If Alaina agreed to be their pet, then she would be cared for in every sense of the word. She would ask for nothing.

Morrisey hadn't felt a need like this in years, even with Amanda, there was the fun of having someone submissive, but there wasn't that longing that he felt with Alaina. She did something to him. Morrisey wasn't sure whether it was because she was naturally submissive or something else. Amanda was good at acting. She played the role of submissive pet, but it was never natural. Alaina, however, her natural state was to submit.

Morrisey watched his brother debate with himself as to what he wanted. He knew that if Cash could get out of his own head, he would fall hard for Alaina. He also believed that Alaina wouldn't tear out Cash's heart like Amanda did. This girl needed love, she needed affection. And she would respond in accord if she had those needs taken care of.

"Let her organize the party, let her see what it is that we desire and if she doesn't go running for the hills, we will discuss it further. I have a feeling though that she will be so intrigued by this life that she will want more," Morrisey said.

Cash looked up at his brother and sighed before shaking his head, "I can't just give my heart, Amanda crushed me, I don't want to live through that again."

Morrisey stepped forward and clasped his hand down on Cash's shoulder giving it a squeeze, "I know Cash, I know. Amanda was a cunt, no doubt about it. Alaina though, she's not like that, I get the feeling she is loyal to a fault and as long as she feels like the queen in our lives, then she will treat us as kings."

Cash nodded and sighed before turning back to his work and typing on the computer. Morrisey wanted to prove to Cash that Alaina was the girl for them. They weren't going to find another girl that would be willing to share so easily and although they hadn't approached Alaina about the prospect of entering the relationship with them, he knew that if she could understand their life, then she would have no issue.

Alaina

Alaina's mind was whirling with thoughts, all night she hadn't been able to get it out of her head, the room behind that secret door. She always knew that she wasn't experienced, she never bothered masturbating, she didn't bother with porn, and any porn she did watch was the vanilla kind, with a man and woman. It just wasn't something she thought of.

That room though, with all the various pieces of equipment and the whips, paddles and whatever the hell that milking machine thing was, sparked her curiosity. She found herself getting more and more excited for the upcoming party as the days wore on.

Her days were filled with planning, cleaning, and cooking for the brothers. She noticed that Morrisey had become somewhat more flirtatious, while Cash watched her like a hawk. Every time she saw him, he had this mindful look on his face as if she were a puzzle that he was trying to figure out. It wasn't that she felt judged by him, or that he was waiting for her to mess up, but more just trying to understand her.

By the time Friday had come around, Alaina was a bundle of nerves. She was apprehensive about the party and what she would see, she hoped that everything she had planned would go off without a hitch. She had made sure to ice bottles of expensive champagne and clean the house to a sparkling state. Alaina had spent all morning making tiny slices to serve. She had spent the afternoon polishing glassware and putting on the finishing touches.

Alaina still had no idea what she was expected to wear to the party or if the brothers even wanted her to be seen. She was lost in thought over that dilemma when Morrisey came into the kitchen wearing a big smile.

"The food smells and looks delicious, and the house has never been cleaner, you've done an amazing job," he gushed.

Alaina smiled and felt her chest puff out with pride as she blushed, "thank you, I just hope that I've done enough."

"I'm sure you have," he said, as he held out a gift bag to her, "I've bought you a gift, something I would like you to wear tonight to the party if you would be willing."

Alaina looked up at Morrisey with wide eyes. His face was filled with excitement as she took the gift bag and looked inside. The first thing she saw was white lace. Alaina gasped as she reached in and pulled out the expensive piece of lingerie. It was the most exquisite item of clothing she had ever owned. Alaina never bothered with expensive lingerie, it was just bras and panties from the department store. Whatever was on sale. However, this piece, this was a luxury.

"I made sure that it covered enough so that it will still be modest, but with your silky skin and beautiful dark hair, it will look gorgeous on you," Morrisey enthused.

"You really want me to wear this? Are you sure?" she asked, she didn't believe that she would look any good in the lingerie. When she held it up, she could see that it was a one piece, that was sheer on the back but, heavy lace decorated the front, so that her nipples and vagina would be covered. Along the sides ran silk ribbons. It really was beautiful; however, Alaina didn't think she could give it the justice that it deserved. She would look like a cheap body clothed in gold; it just wouldn't work.

"I do really want you to wear it, Alaina. You are so beautiful, and I want to show all of our friends, just how beautiful you are and how lucky we are to have you here," Morrisey said with a smile.

Alaina dipped her head, as her face bloomed with embarrassment. She didn't believe that she was beautiful. She didn't think she was ugly, but she was no supermodel. Alaina didn't kid herself that the Caldwell brothers had some gorgeous women that came to their house, and she knew that she would never be able to compare to them.

Morrisey touched Alaina's chin gently, just like he did that first night and lifted her face to look in her eyes, "Alaina you are beautiful, I don't know why no one told you this. I don't know why you feel that you are less than what you are. You are one of the most classically beautiful women I have ever seen, and I would be so honored if you would wear the lingerie that I chose for you and sit with Cash and I during the party."

Alaina gasped and searched Morrisey's face to see if he was telling the truth. "You want me to sit with you and Cash? Who will serve your guests?" she asked.

Morrisey chuckled and ran his thumb along her jaw, "they are grown people, who I'm sure can serve themselves."

Alaina swallowed and sucked in a shuddering breath before nodding. She was going to sit with her bosses while they hosted a party for sex. Her life was about to get interesting.

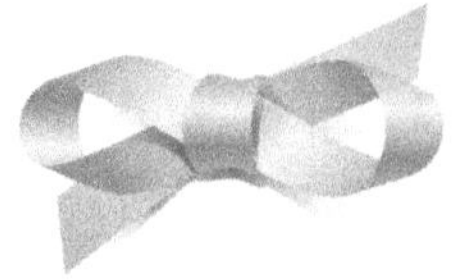

Chapter Six

Alaina's hands were shaking as she stepped out of the steaming shower and wrapped the towel around her body. She couldn't believe what was about to happen. Morrisey and Cash, her reclusive, billionaire bosses, wanted her to wear a lacy piece of lingerie that only covered her vagina and breasts. Her ass was going to be showing to the world, and instead of serving the guests like a housekeeper should, they wanted her to sit with them while their guests partook in all manner of sex.

If anyone had told Alaina this was where her life was going to be last year, she would have laughed so hard that she snorted. She could hardly believe it herself. She swiped over the mirror and looked at herself. Her long dark hair hung down over her shoulders, normally in bouncy waves, but wet it was a mass of curls. Her dark eyes were almost black in color, her tanned skin came from her father's Mediterranean heritage. Her nose was slightly larger than what was considered normal. Something that also came from her father. Her brows were thick, and her eyes were shadowed by long dark eyelashes.

She couldn't see what Morrisey saw in her. He said that she was beautiful, but as Alaina looked at herself in the mirror, she couldn't see it. She didn't think she was ugly; she knew that she wasn't repulsive, she had, had enough interest from boys in the past. Alaina just wasn't interested in them. She had been painfully shy as a teenager, and kept her wall high, to prevent anyone from seeing her weaknesses. The dyslexia made her feel like she was stupid, and she didn't want people to know.

However, there were boys that showed interest despite her high walls she kept around herself. They would tell her that she was hot, they would tell her about how sexy her long legs were and how much they wanted her body. They soon got bored though, when Alaina showed no interest in return. She looked down over her body, her breasts although not huge, were still a good handful, and were perky due to her age. Her legs were long, she stood at five foot ten, another thing she had been self-conscious about when she was a teenager. Alaina had grown fast and early, by the time she was fifteen she was at her full height and towered over some of the boys. That then became another way for girls to tease her.

Morrisey and Cash though were well over six foot, they towered over Alaina and made her feel small and delicate against them. She sighed and shifted her attention to the small piece of lingerie that Morrisey had asked her to wear. She held it up in front of her, the sheer silk on the back felt so soft against her skin, and the lace was beautiful. It highlighted her olive skin.

Determined to let go of her insecurities, Alaina placed the lingerie on the bench and began to get ready for the night. She made a conscious effort to dry and style her hair so that the waves that she normally wore were softer and bouncier than before. Her makeup was smoky, and she stained her lips bright red. When Alaina slipped into the lace lingerie, she started to feel sexy. The feeling of the silk on her back, and the ribbons that ran down her side allowed a new feeling to emerge, something she had never felt before.

Alaina turned and looked at herself in the mirror. Her ass was encased in the sheer fabric and looked good, the material ran high on her hips and over her flat stomach. The lace bralette held her breasts tight and made them sit up even more. Alaina ran her hands down over the fabric, twisting and turning to take in what she looked like. She couldn't help the smile that spread across her face as suddenly she felt sexy, grown up and womanly.

A knock at her bedroom door shook Alaina out of the study of her body. When she opened the door, she saw Morrisey standing in a dark fitted suit on the other side. He gasped when he saw her, his startling green eyes darkening as he took her in.

"You are beautiful," he said with a growl, his voice was husky and instantly made Alaina clench her thighs together to help ease the ache that seemed to be ever present when Morrisey spoke or was in close proximity to her..

Morrisey looked out of this world in his suit, that she knew would have cost more than her weekly pay. His shirt was fitted tight across his muscles, showing off the abs and pecs that were underneath. His pants were tailored to fit beautifully. She wanted to tear off his shirt and lick every inch of his body. Alaina shook her head and looked back up at Morrisey who was watching her with bemusement on his face.

"Are you ready to come and join us, our guests will be here shortly," Morrisey said as he held out his hand for her to take.

Alaina slipped her fingers between his and allowed him to lead her out of the bedroom and down the hall into the kitchen, where she had left all the finger food that she had spent the day preparing. When they got to the kitchen, she saw Cash standing against the bench, with a beer in his hand. His blonde hair was tied back in a man bun, and he wore the same fitted suit that Morrisey wore. Together they were enough to almost cause an orgasm at the sight of them. How women could ever resist she had no idea.

Cash looked over at Alaina and Morrisey as they entered the room and sucked in a sharp breath. He slowly walked towards Alaina and placed his hands gently on her hips. She could feel Morrisey standing behind her, his body pressed against her back, and his hard on pressing against her ass. Cash bent down and ran his nose along Alaina's neck, eliciting a moan from her throat.

"You are beautiful," he whispered huskily into her ear.

Alaina couldn't help but to press back against Morrisey, as her eyes slipped shut. Cash's hands gently glided up her sides, as he continued to run his nose and lips against her neck. Morrisey pushed his erection harder against her and grasped Alaina's hips in a bruising hold. Alaina's breaths were coming in short sharp gasps as the two brothers continued to work her up.

"Are you sure that you want to be our pet tonight?" Cash asked.

Alaina looked up at Cash through hooded lids. She couldn't think beyond the heady feeling of the two men that encased her. Her core was throbbing, and she desperately needed to quench the ache that was like fire between her legs.

"Yes," she said. Alaina had no idea what being a pet to two men would involve, however at that moment she would agree to just about anything.

"Very well. When our guests arrive, they will go directly to our game room. There you will be kneeling between mine and Morrisey's chair. You only speak when we ask you a question or direct you to. You don't move unless we tell you to. Do you understand?" Cash asked, growling into Alaina's ear.

It was a strange request to have her kneel and not tend to their guests, but she was prepared to let go and enjoy the night. When Alaina was in the shower, she had made the decision that she would just go with the flow. If that flow meant that she was to kneel and not speak for the evening, then that is what she would do. Alaina worried what it would mean once the night was over, but she made the decision then and there that she would deal with tomorrow when tomorrow came.

"Yes, I understand," she said.

"One more thing, you will address, Morrisey and I as sir. Do you understand?" Cash spoke again.

Alaina looked up at him through her eyelashes, she couldn't believe what his demanding tone was doing to her. She had never felt so turned on before in her life. "Yes sir, I understand," she said just above a whisper.

"Very good. If at any stage you want this to stop, you say red, if you want us to slow down, you say orange. However, if you say red, you must understand that we stop completely, there will be no going back after that. You will still have your job here, we will not treat you badly, however, there will be no more relationship between the three of us. Do you understand?" Cash explained.

"Yes sir," she said again, feeling more confident with the knowledge that she had an out if it became too overwhelming for her. Cash's reassurance that she would still have her job should she not want to continue with the night helped her to feel empowered in playing along with his requests.

"What are the words?" Cash asked.

"Red to stop, orange to slow down," she repeated.

"Good."

"Sir? Can I ask you a question?" she asked timidly, remembering the rule that she wasn't to speak unless directed to.

Cash raised an eyebrow and shared a look with Morrisey who was still holding her hips in a bruising hold and grinding his erection against her ass.

"Go ahead," Cash said.

"What do you expect of me tonight?" she asked.

"Tonight, will be an introduction into our life. You won't be expected to participate in anything if you aren't wanting to, this will be a chance for you to watch and see what we expect. I can guarantee that Morrisey nor I will ever do anything that will physically damage you. If you agree then there will be an element of pain, however, it comes with immense pleasure and we will only ever go as far as you want to go. We will ask that you try things in the future, that you will step out of your comfort zone. However, tonight, is not about that, tonight is about you watching and deciding if this is a relationship you want to enter," Cash explained.

Alaina was happy that they were giving her the chance to decide if this was something she really wanted, before she jumped in with both feet. Alaina nodded her head and sighed. "Thank you, sir," she said quietly.

Cash gave Alaina's waist a squeeze and smiled, "let's get this food to the room and the champagne poured it will only be a few more minutes before our guests start arriving."

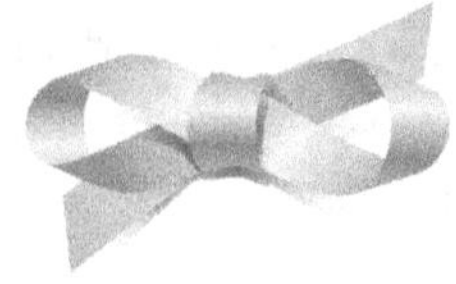

Chapter Seven

Alaina's eyes widened as she entered the room, she didn't want to sound all fifty shades about it, but she didn't know what else to call the room other than a pleasure room or a playroom. However, in that moment, it had changed from when she had seen it with Morrisey. Where Alaina had first thought there was a wall, she now realized that it had been a petition of some sort, that was now folded back to reveal two large, almost throne like chairs against the back wall that was draped with dark red velvet curtains. Between the two thrones was a large deep ruby red cushion.

Cash led Alaina into the room where they placed out the food trays on a table beside the door. Glasses sat along a buffet that was covered in various alcohol while champagne sat in deep ice buckets around the room. The large Saint Andrews cross took up the middle of the room, and two long love seats sat pushed up against the left side. On the other side of the room was the wall of what appeared to be torture devices. Beds that almost looked like massage tables were lined against the right side of the wall under the various equipment.

Alaina saw that to the left as they walked in, there was shelves that she hadn't noticed before that were covered in all various bottles of lube, condoms and massage oils. On the top shelf were unlit candles as well as unopened sex toys. From the roof hung a large chandelier that lit the room in a low light, creating a moody shadow. And from an unseen sound system low instrumental classical music played. The only words that Alaina could find to describe the Caldwell brother's playroom was opulent debauchery.

Cash led Alaina over to the thrones, where he stood in front of the cushion, "this is where you will kneel for the night. A lot of masters expect their sub or pet to bow their head and keep their eyes lowered, Morrisey and I don't expect that of you. We want you to watch. However, should someone approach you, that is when you will lower your eyes, do you understand?"

"Yes, sir," she answered.

"Very good, let's get you settled then," he said as he guided her towards the cushion, that was surprisingly comfortable. Alaina had wondered how she would be on her knees for the length of the party, but as she lowered herself onto the cushion, she realized that the fabric was soft and there was plenty of stuffing to keep her knees from aching.

Cash and Morrisey took their seats in the large darkened thrones. When she looked at them, she realized that they were built from a dark oak wood, and the seat was a black cushion that was built into the chair. They looked like they had been handmade and carved, the workmanship that went into the chair was astounding. Alaina almost snorted as she realized she was kneeling on a cushion, acting as a pet to these two men, about to watch a bunch of strangers have sex and she was busy taking in the workmanship of two damned chairs.

Movement by the door took Alaina's attention and she noticed a small man with a long beard, dressed in nothing but a collar and lead, being led into the room by the most beautiful leggy woman she had ever seen. He was on his knees as he crawled towards where Alaina was knelt between Cash and Morrisey. The woman was dressed in a long leather skirt and corset, her dark hair hung down over her bare shoulders. She looked like she was a Brazilian model. Alaina noticed that the woman also held what looked like a riding crop in one hand.

"Venga, it's wonderful to see you, and you have brought with you a new pet I see," Cash called out cheerfully.

"Cash, yes, this is my latest pet, his name is Jacob," she replied as she walked toward the chairs.

Once Venga was standing in front of Cash and Morrisey, Jacob rubbed his face against Venga's leg as if he were a cat or dog seeking affection. Venga's hand unconsciously ran through Jacob's hair, causing the small man to mewl with contentment. Alaina noticed that as he turned, he had a tail coming from between his ass cheeks. Alaina blushed as she realized that the tail had to be somehow inserted into Jacob's ass.

"Venga's kink is what we call puppy play," Morrisey explained, leaning quietly over to Alaina while Venga and Cash spoke. "It means that Jacob likes to play the part of a puppy or dog, and she is his handler, so he is submissive to Venga."

"May I ask a question sir?" Alaina said quietly to Morrisey.

Morrisey smiled and nodded his head, "I like that you have grasped onto calling us sir so easily, many people don't get that so quickly, but sure what is your question?"

"Is puppy play a sexual thing?" she asked, in her mind she couldn't decide whether it bordered on bestiality. Did it mean that Venga liked to have sex with real dogs, which was disturbing to Alaina and if that was the case, that would be a hard red for her?

"It can be, Venga doesn't have sex with her pups, she just likes the dominance to have them do as she commands. However, others in the kink do have sex with their pups," Morrisey explained. As he took in the frown on Alaina's face he chuckled, "it's not the same as bestiality, they don't want to have sex with real animals, well some might, but none of the ones I've met do. It is more about having that unconditional obedience and submission. Venga is a rarity, in the fact that she is a female handler, most handlers are male, puppy play tends to be more common in the gay kink community, than hetero kink community."

Alaina frowned but nodded her head, she didn't necessarily understand what the appeal was, if they wanted a dog, why not just get a dog, but then she guessed if they were going to have sex, then that made sense to do it with another person. However, no matter if she didn't understand it or not, she wasn't about to shame someone for their choice of kink.

Another couple entered the room, this time it was two men holding hands, they smiled at Cash and Morrisey and gave Venga a small wave. "That is Trent and Ryan. Trent is Ryan's submissive, their relationship is like what Cash and I will have with you, if you choose. Other than the fact that they are two men of course."

"Hello gentlemen," one of the men called out, "I see you have a beautiful new pet."

Trent and Ryan came over to where Morrisey and Cash were seated with Alaina kneeling between them. Alaina lowered her eyes as Cash had instructed her to do if someone were to approach. "She is beautiful, I almost wish I had met her first," Venga said eyeing Alaina and causing her to blush under Venga's scrutiny.

"Ah, we are very lucky indeed," Cash replied as he reached out and threaded his fingers through Alaina's hair causing a shiver to break out through her body.

"Well I'm afraid I don't swing that way; however, your pup, I might be swayed by, Venga," Ryan replied with a chuckle.

Venga ran her hand down over Jacob's head as he smoothed his face onto her leg. "I have been also very lucky. Jacob arrived at the right time," she said with a warm smile, looking down into her pups face and running her fingers under his chin.

Alaina watched the unique relationships between the couples, the more she watched the more she realized that Ryan was the man that was doing the talking, while Trent remained silent. He didn't kneel like Alaina and Jacob, however, he stayed by Ryan's side constantly.

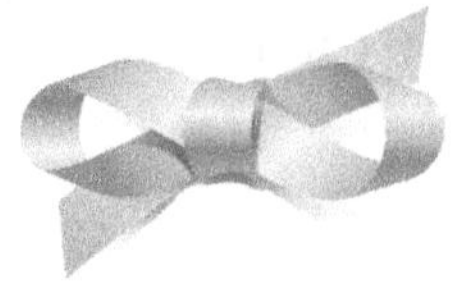

Chapter Eight

It was half an hour later that the room was filled with all kinds of people, who stood around mingling with glasses of champagne and the finger foods that Alaina had made. A short red-haired woman came towards where Alaina was kneeled. She looked at Alaina with narrowed eyes, before she cast her look towards Cash and Morrisey.

"I see the Caldwell brothers replaced Amanda finally, it took you a while," she snorted.

Alaina looked up between Cash and Morrisey to see how they were going to react. Alaina didn't know who Amanda was or why she was replacing her, but from the woman's comment, it seemed that it might have been a sore point. Cash stood from his chair and stormed close to the woman, who shrunk back when he took her by the shoulders.

"Nicole, where is your fucking owner?" Cash snarled, his shoulders were tensed, and Alaina could see him digging his fingers into Nicole's shoulders.

"He, he, let me go," Nicole stammered.

"If you showed him the disrespect that you have just shown my brother and I then I can't say I blame him. I would have thrown your ass out too," Cash growled.

"Amanda was my friend, you can see how I might be upset to see her replaced," Nicole stated, folding her arms across her chest, in a show of bravado.

The more that Alaina looked at her the more she realized just how pretty Nicole was. She was tiny in comparison to Cash, with bright red hair, that made her silky milk like skin shine. Her green eyes flashed in the low light.

"Amanda was a whore who didn't deserve anything we gave her," Cash snarled, he was practically vibrating with anger.

"She was unhappy with the way things were going. You were ignoring her she needed you more Cash. You knew that her sex drive was high when you took up the contract with her, you knew that she couldn't be a kept woman who you just serviced now and then."

Cash threw his head back and roared with laughter. "There were two of us servicing her, twice a fucking day. If we fucked her any more than that she would have formed callouses on her vagina."

Morrisey chuckled, he stood and went towards where Cash still had Nicole in his grasp. Nicole's eyes widened as she saw Morrisey stepping towards her. He leaned down and spoke so quietly that Alaina could only just make out his words.

"I suggest you get the fuck out of my house immediately before I allow Cash to take out every piece of anger and fury that he felt over Amanda on you. Believe me when I say that there will be no pleasure for you."

Nicole nodded her head and took a giant step back, "I'll leave," she said quietly lowering her face to the ground.

"And I suggest you never return here, no matter who your master becomes. You are not welcome in our home," Cash growled.

"I apologize sirs," she said quietly, before quickly turning and almost running for the door.

Morrisey reached out and took Cash by the shoulder and pulled him into his chest, embracing him in a tight hug. Alaina continued to kneel and watch the goings on. It seemed the guests had also noticed the tension, as the conversations ended, and they all watched Morrisey and Cash. Morrisey lifted his head and smiled.

"Let's get this party happening shall we," Morrisey said with a wide smile.

"Yes, lets," a large man in a suit spoke. Alaina recognized him as a local politician that had his face on billboards all over town and adverts on television.

The man led the girl he had beside him. She was a small Asian woman who was naked except for the tight leather collar that was connected to a metal leash that the politician, Stanley, had connected to his wrist. Morrisey and Cash took their seats once again. Cash reached out and ran his fingers through Alaina's hair.

"Come and sit on my lap," Cash said turning his attention to Alaina.

"Yes sir," she said before standing and walking to Cash, who pulled her into his lap. She rested her back against his chest, and he placed a small kiss on her neck, wrapping his arms around her waist and holding her tight against him.

"Stanley loves to strap Ming to the cross, she likes pain more than most, so don't be afraid by what you see, this is the more extreme side of the lifestyle. I don't like to go to the same extremes. Ming has a safe word just like you do, so remember that she is safe, even though what you will see will be a bit frightening," Cash explained quietly into her ear.

Alaina nodded and braced herself for what she was about to witness. Stanley strapped Ming onto the Saint Andrews Cross, her wrists were bound by a leather brace and her ankles were held tight against the wood. Her back was facing where Alaina sat, so she couldn't see Ming's face. But judging by the wetness that Alaina could make out on Ming's thighs, she was excited about what was going to transpire.

Stanley went to the wall of paddles, whips and crops, he picked a large leather whip from the wall, and then went to the shelf of sex toys. He pulled out of the packet a black toy, that Alaina didn't know what it was as well as a long vibrator. She noticed everyone stood around ready for the show that Stanley and Ming were about to perform.

Stanley then used rope to tie the large vibrator between Ming's legs so that the head of the vibrator was on her core. "Are you ready to begin?" Stanley asked.

"Yes sir," Ming replied breathlessly.

"What is our words Ming?" Stanley asked.

"Orange to slow down and red to stop, sir," Ming answered.

"Good girl, do you want to cum sweetheart?" he cooed.

"Yes sir, so badly," she moaned.

Alaina wiggled against Cash's lap and felt his erection start to press against her ass. Her core was throbbing, and she wanted relief. Cash began to slowly run his hands up and down her thighs, not touching where she wanted. Alaina could feel the crotch of her lingerie get wet as she leaned further into Cash, arching her back slightly. Cash ran his fingers gently up and down her sides over the ribbons, stopping just beneath her breasts. Alaina's nipples were hardened pebbles and goose bumps were erupting all over her skin. She wanted to be Ming, at that moment, she wanted everything that the brothers would give her.

Stanley stepped up to Ming and took the black toy that he had selected and covered it in slippery lube. Alaina watched with wonder as he slowly inserted the toy into Ming's ass. She cried out in pleasure and rocked back against him, which made Alaina squirm.

"Are you enjoying this sweetheart?" Cash asked in her ear.

"Yes sir," Alaina panted.

Cash continued his torturous feather light touches up and down her body. Alaina was so focused on Cash's touch that she didn't see Stanley wind his arm back with the whip, until the crack against Ming sounded out with her cry which sounded like a mix between pain and pleasure.

"Oh god," Alaina groaned. She could never imagine that she would have ever been turned on by something that seemed so wrong. Yet watching how Ming responded to everything that Stanley was doing to her, Alaina couldn't fathom anyone thinking this was wrong.

Stanley turned the vibrator on that was wedged between Ming's legs. She cried out and let her knees bend as much as they could pushing her core down tighter on the vibrator attempting to get some relief.

"Don't you cum yet, Ming," Stanley growled.

"Please sir, I'm so close," Ming cried.

"No," Stanley growled, with a crack of the whip against Ming's back.

"Yes," Ming cried, "Oh sir more, please."

Alaina felt herself growing hotter as she wriggled against Cash, her breath was coming out in short sharp bursts. She wanted to cum so badly, she needed relief desperately. Alaina had never felt anything so strong. She didn't think she had a high libido, however, what she was witnessing had her dripping wet.

Cash moved his hands so that his fingers ran along the outside of the lingerie over her crotch. Alaina moaned and threw her head back, closing her eyes. Ming's cries of pleasure and the crack of the whip continued as Alaina focused on Cash's fingers as they danced up and down her body. He slowly slid his fingers over her stomach and up to her chest, before he took her nipples squeezing them hard enough that there was a pinch of pain.

Alaina cried out and wriggled against Cash, the pain added to her pleasure. She needed more. She needed him to touch her between her legs. She needed him to make her cum. Her eyes were shut tight while Cash continued to pinch at her nipples and massage her breasts. She felt another set of hands move her legs so that her thighs were parted. When she looked down, she saw Morrisey looking up at her with a wry smile. He gave her a wink, before he slid the crotch of the lingerie to the side, exposing her folds that she kept waxed clean.

Morrisey groaned as he ran his fingers through her wet folds, "Cash she is so wet for us," Morrisey said with a moan.

"What does she taste like?" Cash asked huskily.

Morrisey bent his head and lapped at her folds, sucking each lip before running his tongue along her clit making her groan and wriggle on Cash's lap. "She tastes like honey, the nectar of the gods," Morrisey moaned.

"Do you need to cum?" Cash asked quietly.

"Yes sir, please, I want to cum," she cried.

That seemed to be all that Morrisey needed to hear as he started to lap at her pussy, sucking her clit into his mouth. He slid two fingers deep inside her. She had never had anyone put anything inside her, not even herself. Alaina ground her pussy against Morrisey's face as she chased that explosion of pleasure. She was so close. Alaina could feel the tingles starting at her spine as it spread up through her chest. Her thighs were shaking, and her toes were curled, as Alaina screamed out her pleasure.

Morrisey continued to suck on Alaina's clit as she cried over and over with erotic pleasure. This was the most amazing feeling she had ever felt. She never wanted it to end.

Chapter Nine

Morrisey

She was so fucking responsive and sensitive to their touch. Morrisey couldn't believe it. His cock was almost bursting at the thought of sinking deep inside her. Even Amanda had never been as responsive as Alaina. Where Amanda's submissive nature was forced, Alaina's was natural. Morrisey couldn't remember the last time he had met a woman who was so naturally submissive. It was every Dom's dream to find a Sub like her, but it rarely was found. Most women thought they wanted submission but had to force their personalities to fully submit to them. Alaina though, she just fell into the role so easily. There was no way he was going to be able to let her go now.

Morrisey just hoped that Cash would feel the same way. As Morrisey looked up at his brothers face, and saw Cash watching Alaina in awe, Morrisey's body relaxed. His brother was just as taken with Alaina as he was. The show between Stanley and Ming continued. Stanley loved to edge Ming for a long time, so he knew there was a lot more to come. Alaina's eyes were opened as she remained relaxed against Cash's chest. Cash continued to gently run his hands up and down her sides. Showing her the love and affection she deserved.

This hadn't been a part of their plan at all. They hadn't intended for Alaina to participate in anything tonight, but just simply watch. Morrisey would have never guessed that she would have gotten comfortable enough for him to expose her to their friends, albeit they weren't watching Alaina. It was a huge step, especially for a woman that was so inexperienced as Alaina.

Morrisey slipped her lingerie back in place so that she was covered and moved up her body, kissing her gently on the lips. He sucked her bottom lip between his teeth and bit down gently, watching her pupils dilate. Morrisey gave her a small smile and a wink.

"That was just a small taste of what would come from us," Morrisey said quietly.

Alaina's breath hitched as she searched his face and a small blush rose on her cheeks. She was truly beautiful, not just because of her innocence, but as a woman she was beautiful.

"Did you enjoy Morrisey's tongue deep in your pussy?" Cash asked her.

Alaina nodded her head and bit her lip. Cash quickly gave her thigh a sharp spank. Nothing to hurt too badly, but enough to leave a small sting and let her know that she had done something wrong. Alaina yelped and turned her head to face Cash. "You need to remember to use your words, Alaina," he said.

Alaina's eyes dropped to the ground, "I'm sorry sir," she said quietly.

Morrisey's eyes widened as he watched the interaction between his brother and Alaina. Cash smiled and took his fingers under her chin, lifting her face to his. "You are forgiven, I'll ask you again, did you enjoy Morrisey's tongue deep in your pussy?" Cash repeated.

"Yes sir," she said with a small smile, another blush blooming on her cheeks.

"I'm glad, would you like to explore more of your sexuality with us Alaina?" Cash asked.

Alaina gave a sharp nod, "yes sir, I would, but I'm not sure that I would be very good for either of you. I don't know what to do."

Alaina dropped her head and looked down at the ground. Morrisey put his hands on her hips and gave them a small squeeze, gaining her attention to him. "Alaina, we don't expect you to be experienced, or know what to do. Part of being a good Dom is teaching you what we expect. It is about showing you just how wonderful and pleasurable sex can be. We want you Alaina, we want all of you and hope that you want all of us too. We will never do anything that you can't handle. And like what has already been explained to you, you are in control. You have the safe words and the minute you choose to use them, that is how Cash and I will respond to you."

Alaina searched Morrisey's face, as she went over everything that he had spoken to her. Morrisey found himself holding his breath waiting for her response. "I'd like to explore more with you both. I would appreciate it if you were to give me a general idea of what I should expect. For example, I see that Ming has got something in her bottom. Is that something you would expect of me?"

Morrisey turned to look at Ming, where she was still strapped to the cross and shaking, begging Stanley to let her orgasm. The vibrator tied between her legs was switched to its highest setting making for a torturous edging session. He noticed that a few others were masturbating while watching, which is something he knew Stanley loved.

"We will talk about that tomorrow. For now, let's continue to watch. I can see that Stanley is getting close to allowing Ming to have her first orgasm. And I imagine that Venga and Jacob will use the milking machine," Morrisey said as they all turned back to watch Ming cry out, begging Stanley.

"You may cum now," Stanley said.

Ming's body sagged as she shook and screamed over and over, her orgasm causing a spray of fluid to release and drip down onto the tiled floor. Behind him, he heard Alaina moan as she watched the woman succumb to the pleasure.

Alaina

The orgasm that had ripped through her body was something she had never experienced and by god she wanted more. And watching Ming reach her own earth-shattering orgasm, flared up the throbbing between Alaina's legs once more. She couldn't hold back the moan that escaped her throat as she wriggled on Cash's lap. His erection was poking her in the ass. She wanted to be able to relieve him but didn't know how or if he would even want that, so, she decided to just sit and wait for him to tell her what he wanted.

Alaina didn't know if it was the atmosphere of the party or whether she was changing, but she was desperate to try this relationship and see where it took her. She had nothing else to lose. Well she had her job, but Cash assured her if she wanted to stop then she would still have her job and home. Although she thought it would be awkward.

By the time Ming was nothing more than a panting mess, and Stanley was unstrapping her from the cross, Venga was leading Jacob to one of the beds lining the wall. Stanley pulled Ming into his arms and cooed into her ear as he carried her over to where the love seat was, he sat down and pulled her into his lap. Ming rested her head on his shoulder, and he stroked her hair lovingly.

Morrisey followed where Alaina was watching the dynamic between Stanley and Ming, "aftercare is very important. Ming having such a huge orgasm is emotional. It takes so much out of her body and her spirit. So, Stanley is strengthening their bond as master and pet."

Alaina liked that, it made her feel better about the idea of entering this arrangement if it meant that they understood that she would need the aftercare like Stanley was giving Ming. Alaina turned her focus onto Venga and Jacob. Venga was strapping Jacob to the bed with leather shackles. She pulled out what looked like a milking machine that you would put on a cow. She took a rubber sheath from a package and put it inside the suction section of the machine.

"Does my puppy want to cum?" Venga cooed to Jacob.

Jacob let out a bark. Alaina had to bite her cheek to stop from laughing, this was going to take a little to get used to. Venga seemed to understand that his bark meant that he wanted to cum. His cock was already erect and standing proudly in the air. Venga squirted some lube onto the head of Jacob's cock allowing it to slowly run down the length and mix with his pubic hair at the base. Venga then reached out and took Jacob's balls in her hand, massaging them lightly. Jacob moaned and threw his head back, arching his hips in pleasure.

Venga chuckled, "does my puppy like that?" she asked. Jacob barked again in response. "Good boy, I'm going to milk every bit of cum out of you. When you cum, I'm going to leave the suction on, and we are going to milk you more. Is my puppy ready for some torture?" Venga asked.

Jacob barked again and nodded his head in response. Venga chuckled as she slowly slid the suction piece down over Jacob's cock. The man moaned and closed his eyes. Venga flicked a switch, causing the machine to start to automatically suck onto Jacobs dick. He groaned and arched his hips again. Venga took Jacob's balls in her hand and started to roll them in her palm.

"Is that machine the same as what they use for cow's sir?" she asked quietly.

Cash chuckled and squeezed her side, "similar, but it specifically made as a sex toy. It works basically the same, it suctions onto the cock and basically jerks it off. Venga is going to make him cum, but she won't stop at just one, she won't turn the machine off until she is satisfied that Jacob has cum many times."

"After a guy cums, his cock is really sensitive, so this is going to hurt Jacob a bit, he will beg for her to stop and cry out, but unless he uses whatever their safe word is, then Venga won't stop until she is ready to," Morrisey explained.

It seemed that sex was far more complexed than Alaina ever knew. She had been taught about sex when she was eleven, just before she started her period. Her mum sat her down and explained the basics of where the man puts his penis. But she never mentioned anything about orgasms, or sex toys. Even masturbation was taboo in their house. She remembers when she accidentally walked in on her brother masturbating. She had no idea what he was doing. When Alaina asked her mum about it later that night, her mum told her that she would have to knock before going into her brother's room and what he did with his body was none of Alaina's business.

It was Kelsey, her best friend, that told her about masturbation. Unlike Alaina, Kelsey grew up with a progressive parent, there were no taboo subjects in Kelsey's house. However, Alaina was always too embarrassed to ask. So instead she just gleamed whatever Kelsey told her. That was how she learned about oral sex. Until that night though, she had no idea just how good it would feel to have a man lick her down there. Just thinking about Morrisey's tongue on her clit made her grind into Cash's lap and squeeze her thighs together.

Jacob's cry of pleasure shook Alaina from her thoughts of Morrisey's tongue, when she looked over at him, he had his head thrown back and was arching his hips, groaning out his orgasm. "That's a good boy, now I want another one," Venga said with a smile.

Jacob shook his head and cried out. He whined and barked, shaking his hips, like he was trying to get the machine off his cock, however, he couldn't. Venga suddenly smacked his leg and growled, "you will take it puppy, or I will punish you."

Jacob whined again before he started panting and moaning, that then led to him screaming out and thrusting his hips.

"Sweetheart, would you be willing to help me cum?" Cash whispered into her ear.

Alaina looked over her shoulder, his green eyes searching hers. "Yes sir," she said biting on her bottom lip. "I don't know what I'm doing though."

"I will teach you," he replied, giving her hips a little shove so that she would stand, "I want you to kneel in front of me."

Alaina dropped to her knees facing Cash. He stood and slipped his pants down along with his boxers, his cock popped out. He was huge. She started to panic, there was no way that was going to fit in her. Her eyes widened and she looked up at Cash.

"It will fit sweetheart, don't worry," he said softly, as he ran his fingers down under her chin.

Alaina simply nodded her head and swallowed. She was going to have to just trust him, but she couldn't imagine something so big fitting inside her. Morrisey had two fingers in her earlier and that was a tight fit as it was. Cash began to stroke his cock slowly up and down. The sight made Alaina's mouth water with lust. A bead of precum bubbled from the head of his cock and started to drip down the shaft. Cash scooped it up and used it to slick the shaft of his cock as he continued to pump his fist.

"Do you want a taste?" Cash asked.

Alaina licked her lips, before she nodded her head. Cash frowned and stopped stroking himself, "words Alaina," he growled.

"Sorry sir, yes I would like a taste," she corrected herself.

"Good girl," Cash said as he slowly reached out and ran his fingers up through her hair, guiding her face towards his cock. "Open your mouth," he said.

Alaina opened her mouth. Cash ran his cock along her bottom lip, she stuck her tongue out and licked the head. Cash moaned and nodded his head, "lick me, taste me," he groaned.

Alaina continued to lick at the head of his cock, tasting the precum that continued to ooze from the end. The taste wasn't something she could describe; it was salty but like nothing she had ever tasted before. It wasn't something she could say that she necessarily liked but she didn't hate it. She continued to lap at Cash's cock as he slowly started to thrust it into her mouth.

Alaina closed her lips around the head of Cash's cock and allowed him to feed more of the shaft into her mouth. Soon he was hitting the back of her throat and making her gag. Her eyes started to water, and she sucked in a deep breath through her nose.

"When it gets to your throat, swallow, it will help open your throat so that you don't gag," Cash said through pants.

On the next thrust when Cash got to her throat she swallowed and felt him go deeper without her gagging. Cash let out a loud groan and began to move his cock in and out of her mouth. Soon he was panting and grunting with his head thrown back and his eyes closed tightly.

"I'm going to cum baby," he groaned, looking down into her eyes.

Without more warning than that, Cash's cock erupted in Alaina's mouth, his cum slid down her throat as she swallowed everything, he gave her. His eyes rolled back and his eyelids slid shut. Cash was crying out her name, his knuckles were white and his fingers tense on his hips. Spurt after spurt Alaina swallowed Cash down, until she felt his cock start to go flaccid in her mouth. She released him with a pop.

Cash opened his eyes and looked down at her with so much affection it made Alaina's heart jump. "Thank you beautiful girl," he said running his fingers under her chin. He gave her a wink and tucked his cock back in his pants.

"Come kneel on your cushion again and watch some more," Cash said, holding his hand out to her to take.

She stood and Cash led her back to her cushion that she had started kneeling on at the beginning of the night. Alaina turned her attention back to Jacob and Venga. She had turned the machine off and was telling him what a good boy he was. While another woman led a man that Alaina hadn't met to the cross and began to strap him in.

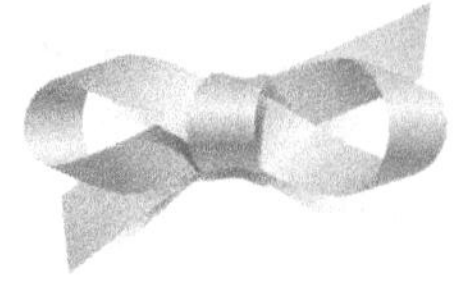

Chapter Ten

Alaina continued to watch the couples as they played with various sex toys, whips, ties and feathers. She was in complete awe by it all. Morrisey didn't touch her again and Cash seemed happy to continue to stroke his fingers through her hair as she kneeled beside him. By the time the night wrapped up she was exhausted, but her pussy was throbbing with need. The orgasm that Morrisey had given her was intense and she enjoyed it, however, she wanted more.

Once all the guests left, and she had finished stacking the dishwasher with glassware and serving platters, Alaina dragged herself to her bedroom to run a hot bath and maybe replicate some of what Morrisey had done to her. By the time the bathroom was full of steam and Alaina was soaked under the water she let her fingers roam down over her body, touching her breasts and tugging at her pebbled nipples imitating what Cash had done to her.

Slowly she slid her fingers down over her mound and through her folds that felt slick even in the water, until she found that bundle of nerves that had brought her so much pleasure. Alaina experimented with different touches, between pinching, circling her fingers, as well as alternating between fast and slow strokes. Soon she was panting and writhing in the bath. She was so caught up in her pleasure that she hadn't heard Cash enter the bathroom, and it wasn't until she felt his hand take hold of her wrist and replace her fingers with his, that she even realized that she was no longer alone.

Alaina's eyes widened and he gave her a small smile. "How about you get out of the bath and I take you to bed, I will fill you, and give you even more pleasure than just your fingers could give," he crooned.

Alaina nodded her head, which made him raise his eyebrow. "Yes sir," she said quietly as she fumbled for the bath plug and stood from the steaming water and stepped into the towel that he held out for her.

Once Alaina was wrapped in the towel, she followed Cash into her bedroom. He turned and pulled her into him, taking her lips in a bruising kiss that set her whole body on fire. She was practically vibrating with need. Their tongues danced together while his hands grasped at her ass and pulled her in tight against him. Cash's cock was pressed hard against her belly. She needed him.

"I'm going to make love to you. We aren't going to do any of what you saw tonight, not right now, I just want to be deep inside you. I want to feel your whole-body quake underneath me. I want to listen to you cry out my name as you cum," he growled as he laid her down onto the bed and unfolded the towel from around her.

Alaina was panting as she watched with hooded lids while he slowly stripped from his shirt, revealing the hard muscle that she already knew would be hidden there. Cash kept eye contact the entire time he stripped from his clothes slowly and then gently widened her legs. Taking her thighs in his big hands he lifted her hips and hooked her feet over his back.

Cash leaned forward kissing her passionately again. Alaina felt his erection at her entrance as he swiveled his hips and ran the head of his cock through her folds. A rush of panic gripped her as she realized that this was it, she was about to lose her virginity, to not only a man she hardly knew but her boss as well. All the implications of her choice flooded her mind.

Cash took her chin and touched it gently, "we move at your pace, I promise not to hurt you," he said quietly.

Alaina bit her lip as she nodded her head, forcing her body to relax. Once Cash could see her mind was calm, he slowly moved his cock inside her. The pinch of pain caused Alaina to suck in a breath, but it wasn't something that was too painful to deal with. Cash paused and waited for her to be able to accommodate his size, before he slowly started to move in and out of her.

The feeling was like nothing she had ever experienced, she felt so full it was almost overwhelming and the pleasure that built between her legs had her crying out and lifting her hips to meet his every thrust. It didn't take long for Alaina to feel the first tingles of her approaching orgasm. She knew this was going to be bigger than her first, her eyes rolled back, and her lids closed on their own accord.

"Alaina, look at me," Cash growled.

Alaina's eyes snapped open and she stared up into the darkened green eyes of Cash as her orgasm washed over her taking her to heights she had never been before. She screamed out over and over as Cash continued to thrust deep inside her, pulling her pleasure out for longer. His breathing became staggered and he groaned as he thrust harder chasing his own orgasm. Finally, he found his pleasure and followed her over the line.

They lay panting, wrapped in each other's arms, sweat slickened their exhausted bodies. Alaina's eyes were drifting closed, as she felt Cash gently pull out of her. "Come hop up and into bed," he whispered.

Half asleep Alaina climbed off the bed and slid between her sheets, her head had hardly hit the pillow before she was already sound asleep.

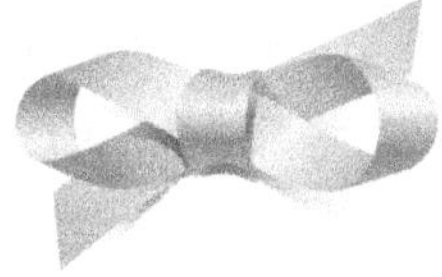

Chapter Eleven

When Alaina's alarm sounded in the morning, she woke up encased in a pair of arms. She couldn't wipe away the small smile that spread across her lips as she remembered the night before and the pleasure that Cash seemed to be able to pull from her body. Alaina felt lips caress small kisses across the back of her neck and down over her shoulder and rolling she found herself looking into Cash's eyes.

"Morning beautiful," he said, his voice husky from sleep.

"Good morning sir," she replied, lowering her eyes before quickly looking back up at him.

Cash's lips quirked and he kissed her gently, running his hands down over her sides. She was still naked from the night before and could feel her body aching in all the right places. Cash pushed his hips towards her, grinding his erection into her stomach. Alaina moaned, feeling herself get wet with excitement.

Cash's kisses became more fervent, as his tongue slid along hers. The door opened and looking over Cash's shoulder she saw Morrisey enter with a broad smile. "Well now, this is a sight I like to see," he chuckled, causing Alaina to giggle.

Morrisey rounded the bed, slipping off his clothes as he went, before sliding into the sheets behind Alaina and circling his arm over her waist. He pressed open mouthed kisses along her neck and shoulders, pushing his erection into her ass. Alaina was panting with excitement as the two brothers wound her up higher. Cash slid his hand down over her thigh and lifted her leg, so that it was hooked over Morrisey's hip.

Like a coordinated dance Morrisey slipped inside her, while Cash continued to kiss her bruised lips. Alaina groaned as she felt Morrisey slide his way deep inside, hitting the most intense area she had ever felt. Every movement over that one spot had her body shuddering under the weight of her pleasure. She was crying out and felt her legs quaking.

Cash slid his fingers down over her stomach and flicked them over her swollen clit, it was all it took before she was screaming incoherent words, thrusting herself back harder onto Morrisey's cock. Morrisey continued to move deep inside her, while Cash didn't let up the ministrations on her clit. It was almost too much pressure as the feeling in her sensitive bud became heightened.

Alaina's eyes widened and she looked up at Cash, she debated whether now was the right time to cry out the word orange, but the look on his face, said that he was completely in control and knew what he was doing. Without warning an orgasm that was almost painful washed over her, stars floated in front of her eyes, somewhere in the distance she heard Morrisey cry out her name and fill her with his fluids. She was gasping for air; her voice was hoarse and her whole body was covered in a sheen of sweat. However, she wanted more, she didn't want it to end. When she felt Morrisey slip from her folds she cried out at the loss of fullness he created inside her.

However, she wasn't empty for long as Cash slid in where his brother had left. Alaina moaned at the feeling and buried her face into the crook of Cash's neck. He slowly started to move inside her, he seemed in no hurry to get to the destination and Alaina was happy to go along for the ride. By the time she had succumb to her fourth orgasm, Cash cried out her name and filled her with his seed. He kissed her long and hard, running his hands through her hair.

"Oh, my goodness," she said quietly.

Cash smirked, while Morrisey chuckled behind her, "do you think you can do that regularly?" Morrisey asked.

"I'm willing to give it a try," she answered.

"That's all I ask," Cash chuckled, tapping her on the hip, before rolling out of the bed.

Alaina watched him move towards the bathroom, his body was like that of a Greek Adonis. He was beautiful. He was covered in muscle, his firm ass, she wanted to kiss and bite. She had never thought of herself as an overly sexual woman, however, now lying in the bed watching one of her men, her boss, walk towards her bathroom she could see she was quickly becoming addicted.

"What happens now?" she asked Morrisey quietly, rolling to look at him.

He was lying on his back, with his arm slung over his eyes. "What do you mean?" he asked, as he moved his arm to look over at her.

"She means, where do we go from here, what is the status of our relationship?" Cash answered from the door.

That was exactly what she meant. Was she still just an employee that the brothers slept with when they felt like it, or when they had a party? Or was she their girlfriend. And if she was their girlfriend, what was she going to do for money? Suddenly her snap decision to get involved with the Caldwell brothers on more than an employee relationship didn't seem to be her brightest idea.

"You are ours," Morrisey answered, as if that just fixed all her concerns.

"What does that mean though?" she asked, sitting up and taking the sheet with her to cover her breasts.

Cash came and sat on the end of the bed, tugging the sheet from her hands to expose her chest. "It means that you are our partner or girlfriend, whatever label you want to put on it."

"But what about working for you? I can't afford to not have a job," she said as her brows pinched together.

"We don't expect you to have nothing. If you continued to do what you were doing as an employee then we will continue to pay you, if that is what you want. If it were my choice you would live here and allow my brother and I to spoil you and give you everything you need, however, we understand that something like that isn't an easy decision to make," Cash explained.

Alaina nodded and sighed, "it wouldn't be an easy decision for me to make. My family are working class people, I didn't grow up with everything being handed to me. We always worked for what we had, so for me to just accept you giving me everything, I'm not sure that I would be comfortable with it."

"That's fine. How about we continue to pay you, as the relationship matures, then we can later come back to this. There is something that I want to do though. I want to have you work with us a contract," Cash said.

"A contract?" Alaina questioned; she was envisioning something like the N.D.A she signed when she first started working with the brothers.

"It sounds formal but it's more a way for us to know where your hard limits are and where we can push a little, for example, you might have a hard limit that you aren't willing to get a clitoral hood piercing, however, you might be willing to in the future try anal. Then there will be things that you are willing to do, like spankings for example or orgasm control, it is just a way for us to know where your limits lie. The last thing we want is for you to have to use your safe word and this relationship to stop. So, if we have a contract in place, it allows us to know what you are willing to do, and it's a good way for you to know what we expect of you," Morrisey explained.

All of that sounded fair to Alaina, although she wasn't sure that she could ever put anal on her willing to try in the future list. She bit her lip and nodded her head, "okay, I think a contract is a good idea, that would make me feel a lot more comfortable."

"Good, well why don't you go and have a shower, while Morrisey and I go and get cleaned up and then we can all sit down and have breakfast. Then later this afternoon we will create the contract together," Cash said, tapping her ankle and encouraging her to get out of bed.

Alaina climbed out of bed and headed towards the bathroom; her muscles cried out from being used in ways that they had never been used before.

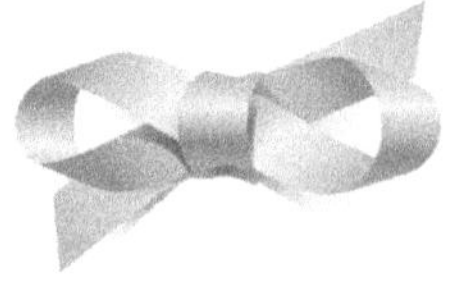

Chapter Twelve

Once Alaina finished cleaning the kitchen after a breakfast of pancakes, bacon and fruit, she went in search of the brothers. Cash had explained that they were going to the office and would write out their expectations of the contract. Alaina suspected that they already had their part written out. What was going to be in the final contract would be what she wanted to input. The concept made her nervous. She wasn't someone who had spent any time thinking about sex other than one day in the long distant future. She had never even given the idea of spankings and god forbid anal any thought at all.

Knocking on the door of the office, she felt her nerves start to kick about in her stomach. Alaina bit her lip and waited to hear permission to enter. She really enjoyed what she had witnessed the night before, she had most definitely enjoyed what she had experienced the night before and then again that morning. However, knowing that what happened to her was pretty vanilla in comparison to what the brothers intended made her question whether she was ready for anything like this.

"Come in," Morrisey called out.

When Alaina went into the room Cash and Morrisey had some papers sitting on the desk in front of them. Glancing down she could see her name at the top and a declaration of some sort. She bit her lip and sucked in a deep breath trying to will herself not to run, but instead to enjoy what it might be.

"Alright, so this is a list of things that we would like from our pet. What we need from you is to go through the list, and really think about it, don't just cast something off because it seems like it could be out of your comfort zone. Really think whether you would be willing to try. I want you to put a cross next to everything you would flat out refuse, a question mark next to what you might try but aren't sure you would like and a tick beside everything that you would willingly submit to," Cash explained, as he handed Alaina the list.

Alaina's eyes widened when she realized the list didn't just consist of one page yet many pages. Skimming through what was written, she started to feel even more terrified, when she noticed words like fisting, both vaginally and anally. There was no way she could do something like that. Or could she? Is it something that is pleasurable?

"Why don't you take it back to your room and read through the list and bring it back to us when you've finished?" Morrisey said with a smile.

Alaina nodded her head and took the papers in her shaking hands as she left the room. She sat on her bed looking through the various sexual acts that the brothers would expect of her. Alaina chewed on her lip. Was she really brave enough to be able to do this? As she looked through the list, she questioned each act, spankings, yes, she could do and would happily try, kneeling, well she had no problem with that. Anal she was still on the fence about, butt plugs, was the same. Fisting was a hard no. And what the hell was candle play?

The more she read through the list the more questions she had. Alaina stood from her bed, determined to seek the brothers out again. She knocked on the door to the office and heard Cash respond with what sounded like humor in his voice. When she opened the door, both the Caldwell brothers were looking at her with broad smiles, as if they had expected her to return.

"I have some questions," she said.

"We thought you might," Morrisey chuckled.

"Why don't we go through the list together?" Cash suggested.

Alaina nodded her head and put the pieces of paper on the desk in front of her, Morrisey and Cash looked at the ones that she had already put ticks beside. "Well you have made a good start, spankings, feather play, blindfolds, orgasm control and vibrators are all fairly tame. I can see that you've put a question mark next to Shibari, the Japanese rope work, anal and butt plugs. Yet you've put a cross beside fisting, so what are your concerns?" Cash asked.

"I don't know what candle play is for a start," she said.

"Ah, well, candle play is using a special wax to pour over the skin, normally the nipples, once the wax dries, it makes the nipples a lot more sensitive to touch," Morrisey explained.

"And that is something you like doing?" she asked.

Morrisey gave her a wry smile and nodded, "I like everything that is on that list."

Alaina sighed, "I don't know how much I'm ready for. I mean, I had sex for the very first-time last night, if we count all the times, I've had sex it's a great big three. I don't know if I'm ready to explore my sexuality that deeply."

"We don't expect you to do everything on the list straight away. Alaina, we aren't going to expect you to move too quickly, each introduction will be slow and controlled, we would start with the more vanilla things, such as blind folding, feather play, and then we can work our way up to the more extreme. The main thing about this sort of relationship is trust. We want you to trust us. We want to know that you trust Cash and I with your pleasure, knowing that we will never push you beyond what you are ready for," Morrisey explained.

"We don't take our role of master lightly. We know how much faith it takes for a pet to put their trust in us. We know to the outside world this may be even seen as abusive. However, the last thing we ever want to do is cause you pain, that is not followed by pleasure or to make you feel afraid or uncomfortable around us. This is about you. You are the queen in this situation. Although you are submissive to us, you rule the relationship. You are the one with the safe word. You are the one that says when enough is enough, you are the one that has the choice of when to end it. Therefore, this contract is so important. We need to make sure that you are completely comfortable enough to trust us," Cash explained.

When he explained it that way, it made more sense. Suddenly the relationship didn't seem as overwhelming. She began to feel empowered. It was true in fact she did hold all the power of the relationship, not the other way around. She did have her safe word, and should she choose to use it, then the brothers would stop the relationship immediately. Emboldened by Cash's words she gave an assertive nod of her head and sucked in a deep breath.

"Alright, I can do this," she said as she looked down at the paper in front of her.

"Great, now let's go through this list and work together to find what you are comfortable with," Morrisey said with a wicked grin.

He seemed to be enjoying this a lot. Alaina giggled and shook her head, taking the list and starting to read through. She continued to ask about various acts on the list and the brothers continued to explain to her what was involved. She was still a hard no when it came to fisting, well anally at least. The more they explained, the more she decided that maybe she would give the vaginal fisting a go, in the future, a very far and distant future.

"I think I'd like to try everything once, however, if I don't like something, I will let you know," she said once they had finished going through the list.

"That's all we will ever ask of you sweetheart," Cash said with a smile as he leaned over and kissed her gently on the lips.

Morrisey's eyes played with happiness. And so, began her new life.

The end... For Now, ...

Don't miss out!

Visit the website below and you can sign up to receive emails whenever S L Davies publishes a new book. There's no charge and no obligation.

https://books2read.com/r/B-A-NZRR-RFJDC

BOOKS2READ

Connecting independent readers to independent writers.

Did you love *Maid for the Doms*? Then you should read *Freya*[1] by S L Davies!

Freya had been working at Club KINK since she was eighteen years old. Having grown up in the foster care system she was grateful to find a place that she finally belonged and to create a family that was hers. Not to mention learning about her kinks as Domme.

Miles wasn't out of the loop when it came to kink. He knew he was submissive, but he hadn't had the chance to play. Mainly because he'd never found a place he was comfortable to let go. But when the vampire Domme Freya took his eye, he knew, not only was she someone he could trust with his whole heart and soul, she was his mate. But Freya wasn't someone that would be a one man woman, no this vampire was someone to be shared.

---

1. https://books2read.com/u/4jqWko

2. https://books2read.com/u/4jqWko

Caden and Creed had moved to Lalbert in hopes of a new life, away from the drama that their parents had left behind. When they discovered Club KINK, they knew instantly they would give it a go. They never expected that they would find a new home.

This is an Reverse Harem, with triggering subjects. The kink is dominance and submission, as well as blood play and cbt. Language and themes suited to 18+

KINK Series
Book One: Freya (Blood Play)
Book Two: Tanquil (Cum Play)
Book Three: Gunner (Puppy Play)
Book Four: Newlyn (Feederism)
Book Five: Aina (Sadomasochism)
Book Six: Ione (Age Play)
Read more at https://www.amazon.com/~/e/B0832T8F7Z.

Also by S L Davies

Breeding Facility
Memphis
Bacchus
Coltrane
Pax
Raiden
Nash
Breeding Facility

Devil's Advocates
Lynx
Israel
Jai
Jasper
Arley
Zion
Oakland

KINK
Gunner

Newlyn
Aina
Freya
Tanquil

Obsidian Mechanics
Donte
Atticus
Boden

Onyx Rebels
Onyx Rebels Prologue
Hawke
Rison
Bandit
Butler
Nova

Rigby Brothers
Asher
Burgess
Macklin
Drake
Jericho
Obsidian

Schiavu
Schiavu

Shifter Ink
Brenton
Chase
Orion
Sloane

Stolen
Stolen
The Murphy Princess
Little Warrior

Wild Claw Pack
Connell

Standalone
Sisters Revenge
Killer Love
Soldiers At War
Second Chances
Bunny
Caged

By The Sword
The Cult
Rising Sun
Forbidden Bound
Christmas Escape
Executioner
Maid for the Doms

Watch for more at https://www.amazon.com/~/e/B0832T8F7Z.

About the Author

S L Davies is an Australian Author living in Country, Victoria. She is inspired by the world around her.

Read more at https://www.amazon.com/~/e/B0832T8F7Z.

9 7 9 8 2 1 5 7 7 3 2 8 4